CoComelon™

I'M A FIREFIGHTER!

Adapted by May Nakamura

SIMON SPOTLIGHT
New York London Toronto Sydney New Delhi

SIMON SPOTLIGHT
An imprint of Simon & Schuster Children's Publishing Division
1230 Avenue of the Americas, New York, New York 10020
This Simon Spotlight edition December 2022
CoComelon™ & © 2022 Moonbug Entertainment. All Rights Reserved.
All rights reserved, including the right of reproduction in whole or in part in any form.
SIMON SPOTLIGHT and colophon are registered trademarks of Simon & Schuster, Inc.
For information about special discounts for bulk purchases, please contact Simon & Schuster Special Sales at
1-866-506-1949 or business@simonandschuster.com.
Manufactured in the United States of America 1122 LAK
10 9 8 7 6 5 4 3 2 1
ISBN 978-1-6659-2743-7
ISBN 978-1-6659-2744-4 (ebook)

JJ and his friends have a special visitor at school today. Who could it be? JJ can't wait to find out!

"That's right—I'm a firefighter!"

Nina's mom is here to teach JJ and his friends about staying safe in case of a fire at their school. Firefighters are important helpers!

Nina runs over to give her mom a hug and sings,

"I'm going to be a firefighter!"

Let's wear a bright red fire hat,
a shiny bright red fire hat.

Nina's mom wears a red fire hat that protects her head while she works. She wears the hat every day, just like JJ wears his helmet every time he rides his tricycle or scooter.

In a bright red fire hat,
I look like a firefighter.
Wee-ooh! Wee-ooh!

JJ and Nina think fire hats look bright and fun.

♫ Let's wear a yellow fire coat,
a big and yellow fire coat. ♩

Nina's mom also wears a fire coat. It's made from special materials, so her coat won't burn easily, even if flames touch it.

The coat also has bright stripes. The stripes help people see firefighters through smoke during a fire, and they also help people driving cars at night see firefighters on the road.

"Look at me!" Cody says, trying on a pretend fire coat.

In a yellow fire coat,
I look like a firefighter.
Wee-ooh! Wee-ooh!

Ms. Appleberry pulls out a pretend fire engine. It has a lot of wheels, and white ladders to reach tall places.

Let's get in the fire engine, a big, red, shiny fire engine.

Nico and Bella get in the fire engine and pretend to ride around. "Fire engine coming through! Keep the streets clear!" Bella says.

In a big red fire engine,
I look like a firefighter.
Wee-ooh! Wee-ooh!

Nina's mom places a pretend fire in the corner of the classroom. "Oh no, there's a fire!" she says.

What will JJ and his friends do?

Fire hoses are very long so they can reach almost anywhere . . . even tall buildings! Everyone works together to bring the hose closer to the imaginary fire.

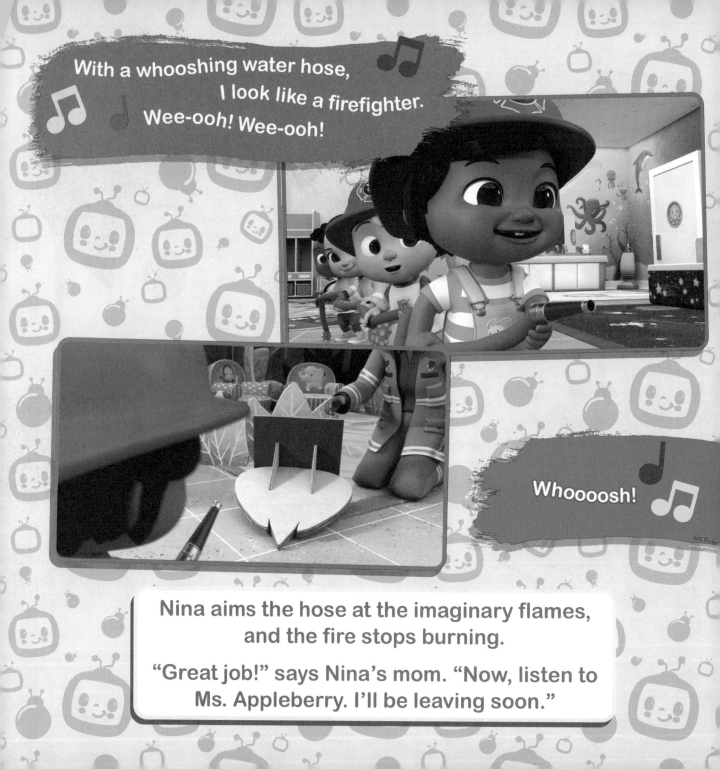

With a whooshing water hose,
I look like a firefighter.
Wee-ooh! Wee-ooh!

Whoooosh!

Nina aims the hose at the imaginary flames,
and the fire stops burning.

"Great job!" says Nina's mom. "Now, listen to
Ms. Appleberry. I'll be leaving soon."

WHOOP! WHOOP! WHOOP! 🎵

Suddenly the fire alarm on the classroom wall starts to ring. It flashes a bright red light. What is happening now?

In a drill, there is no real fire. JJ and his friends
pretend that there is a fire so they will know
what to do if there is ever a fire at school.

JJ stays calm and listens to Ms. Appleberry's directions. "Line up and follow me outside," Ms. Appleberry says.

One by one, JJ and his friends leave the classroom and move away from the building.

Ms. Appleberry takes roll call to make sure everyone is in line and safe.

"JJ?" says Ms. Appleberry.

"Here!" says JJ.

"Nina?" says Ms. Appleberry.

"Here!" says Nina.

Nina's mom looks to make sure there is no fire in the school. She also checks whether anyone is in danger.

"Everything looks good!" she says.

JJ feels safe knowing that Ms. Appleberry and Nina's mom are here to help during a fire.

"When I grow up, I want to be a brave firefighter and help people, just like you do!" Nina says to her mom.

"You will be a great firefighter!" her mom says.